Eddie the Elephant

Stephanie Jeffs
Illustrated by Steve Hicks

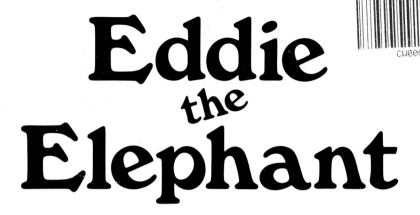

A TAMARIND BOOK

Young Eddie was an elephant
With tail behind and trunk in front.
But Eddie, I regret to say,
Wished he'd been made another way.

5

A little thought popped in Ed's mind,
A nagging thought, the lasting kind.
'If I looked different, I am sure
My friends would like me even more!'

That night when Eddie tried to sleep,
He tossed and turned and counted sheep.
Although at last his eyes shut tight
His mind went racing through the night.

Young Eddie dreamed that it was day
And he was with his friends at play.
He tried to run – but not a hope,
And then he saw an antelope.

'Oh how I wish,' poor Eddie cried,
'That I could run like him!' He tried!
To his surprise he found he could!
His legs had changed – he knew they would!

'Yippee!' cried Ed, 'I'm running free!
But this is not enough for me.
My trunk can change, I know it can.
Give me a beak like a pelican!'

Within a flash his trunk was gone
And Eddie thought, 'What have I done?
My legs are fine, my beak's all right,
My back – well that's an awful sight!'

'Now what I need,' continued Ed,
'Is something higher than my head.
A camel's hump would do the trick.
Please give me one, and make it quick!'

As Eddie spoke two humps appeared
And even Eddie thought them weird!
'One would have done,' he said aloud,
'But there again – I'm not that proud.'

The two humps stayed. He looked a sight.
But Eddie thought they looked just right.
'Just one more try or maybe two,'
Thought Eddie, 'then I think I'm through.'

He racked his brain: what could he add?
And now our Eddie looked quite sad.
'Perhaps some fins – no that's absurd.
I know, I'll have wings like a bird.'

The wings appeared and flapped out wide.
'Now I'm done!' Ed said with pride.
'At last the new transform-Ed me!
Quick everybody! Come and see!'

And in his dream the new Ed stood,
The wonder of the neighbourhood.
A crowd had gathered just to see
How Ed had changed so totally.

Before his friends he flew and ran,
Shrugged humps, ate fish like a pelican.

Sang Ed, 'I hope you like me more
Now I look different from before!'

Then several silent minutes passed.
'What do you think?' said Ed at last.
'Well to be honest, Ed,' they said,
'We think you've gone soft in the head!'

'But don't you like me even more
Now I look different from before?'
Cried Eddie. 'No!' his friends all said,
'Bring back Eddie, we want old Ed!'

Poor Eddie woke and sat upright.
His dream had given him a fright!

He looked and was relieved to find
Just trunk in front and tail behind!

So if like Ed you ever find
A little thought pops in your mind,
Be warned! Remember foolish Ed
(Whose friends thought he'd gone off his head)

And in your thoughts remember God,
Who does not think that you look odd,
But planned you in particular
And loves you just the way you are!

A Tamarind Book
Published in association with SU Publishing
130 City Road, London EC1V 2NJ
ISBN 1 873824 02 5

First edition 1993

Copyright © 1993 AD Publishing Services Ltd
Text copyright © 1993 Stephanie Jeffs
Illustrations copyright © 1993 Steve Hicks

Printed and bound in Singapore